J636.73
GRE
C.1

DOG BREEDS
Boxers

by Sara Green

Consultant:
Michael Leuthner, D.V.M.
PetCare Clinic, Madison, Wisc.

BELLWETHER MEDIA • MINNEAPOLIS, MN

J636
.73
GRE
c.1

Note to Librarians, Teachers, and Parents:

Blastoff! Readers are carefully developed by literacy experts and combine standards-based content with developmentally appropriate text.

Level 1 provides the most support through repetition of high-frequency words, light text, predictable sentence patterns, and strong visual support.

Level 2 offers early readers a bit more challenge through varied simple sentences, increased text load, and less repetition of high-frequency words.

Level 3 advances early-fluent readers toward fluency through increased text and concept load, less reliance on visuals, longer sentences, and more literary language.

Level 4 builds reading stamina by providing more text per page, increased use of punctuation, greater variation in sentence patterns, and increasingly challenging vocabulary.

Level 5 encourages children to move from "learning to read" to "reading to learn" by providing even more text, varied writing styles, and less familiar topics.

Whichever book is right for your reader, Blastoff! Readers are the perfect books to build confidence and encourage a love of reading that will last a lifetime!

This edition first published in 2009 by Bellwether Media.

No part of this publication may be reproduced in whole or in part without written permission of the publisher. For information regarding permission, write to Bellwether Media Inc., Attention: Permissions Department, Post Office Box 19349, Minneapolis, MN 55419-0349.

Library of Congress Cataloging-in-Publication Data
Green, Sara, 1964-
   Boxers / by Sara Green.
     p. cm. – (Blastoff! readers. Dog breeds)
   Includes bibliographical references and index.
   Summary: "Simple text and full color photographs introduce beginning readers to the characteristics of the dog breed Boxers. Developed by literacy experts for students in kindergarten through third grade"–Provided by publisher.
   ISBN-13: 978-1-60014-219-2 (hardcover : alk. paper)
   ISBN-10: 1-60014-219-2 (hardcover : alk. paper)
   1. Boxer (Dog breed)–Juvenile literature. I. Title.

SF429.B75G74 2008
636.73–dc22
                                       2008019993

Text copyright © 2009 by Bellwether Media, Inc. BLASTOFF! READERS and associated logos are trademarks and/or registered trademarks of Bellwether Media Inc.

SCHOLASTIC, CHILDREN'S PRESS, and associated logos are trademarks and/or registered trademarks of Scholastic Inc. Printed in the United States of America.

Contents

What Are Boxers?	4
History of Boxers	10
Boxers Today	16
Glossary	22
To Learn More	23
Index	24

What Are Boxers?

When you first see a Boxer, you will probably see a tough-looking dog. If you get to know one, you are likely to find a very playful dog too. Boxers can make great pets. They can also be helpful to people.

Adult Boxers weigh between 55 and 70 pounds (25 and 32 kilograms). They are between 21.5 and 25 inches (54.6 and 63 centimeters) tall.

Most Boxers have smooth **coats** that are **fawn** or **brindle** in color.

Many Boxers have white marks on their coats. White marks are called flash. Boxers with white marks on their face are called flashy.

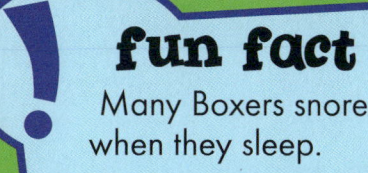
fun fact
Many Boxers snore when they sleep.

Boxers are born with floppy ears. **Veterinarians** can give dogs an operation to make their ears stand up. However, many owners choose to keep their Boxer's ears floppy.

Boxers are sensitive to very hot or cold weather. Their short hair does not keep them warm in cold weather. Boxers have short **muzzles**. This means they have short **airways**. That makes it harder for them to cool down by **panting** in hot weather.

History of Boxers

The **ancestors** of the Boxer **breed** lived in Europe a few hundred years ago. One breed was called Bullenbeissers. They were brindle in color and had floppy ears.

Bullenbeissers were large and strong, with powerful jaws. They made excellent hunting dogs. People used them to hunt boars. Boars had sharp teeth and fought hard, but Bullenbeissers were strong enough to handle them.

Bullenbeisser

Two other ancestors of the Boxer are the English Bulldog and the Mastiff. English Bulldogs are short, sturdy dogs with white markings. They were popular hunting dogs in Germany. Mastiffs are large, powerful dogs. They make great guard dogs.

English Bulldog

Mastiff

Over time, Bullenbeissers, English Bulldogs, and Mastiffs had puppies together. These puppies were the first Boxers. English Bulldogs and Mastiffs are still popular pets, but Bullenbeissers are **extinct**.

Boxers were very important during World War I and World War II. They carried messages and equipment for soldiers. Some of these soldiers came to think of their Boxers as pets.

Many World War II soldiers brought their Boxers back home to the United States when the war ended. Boxers soon became very popular pets in the United States.

Boxers Today

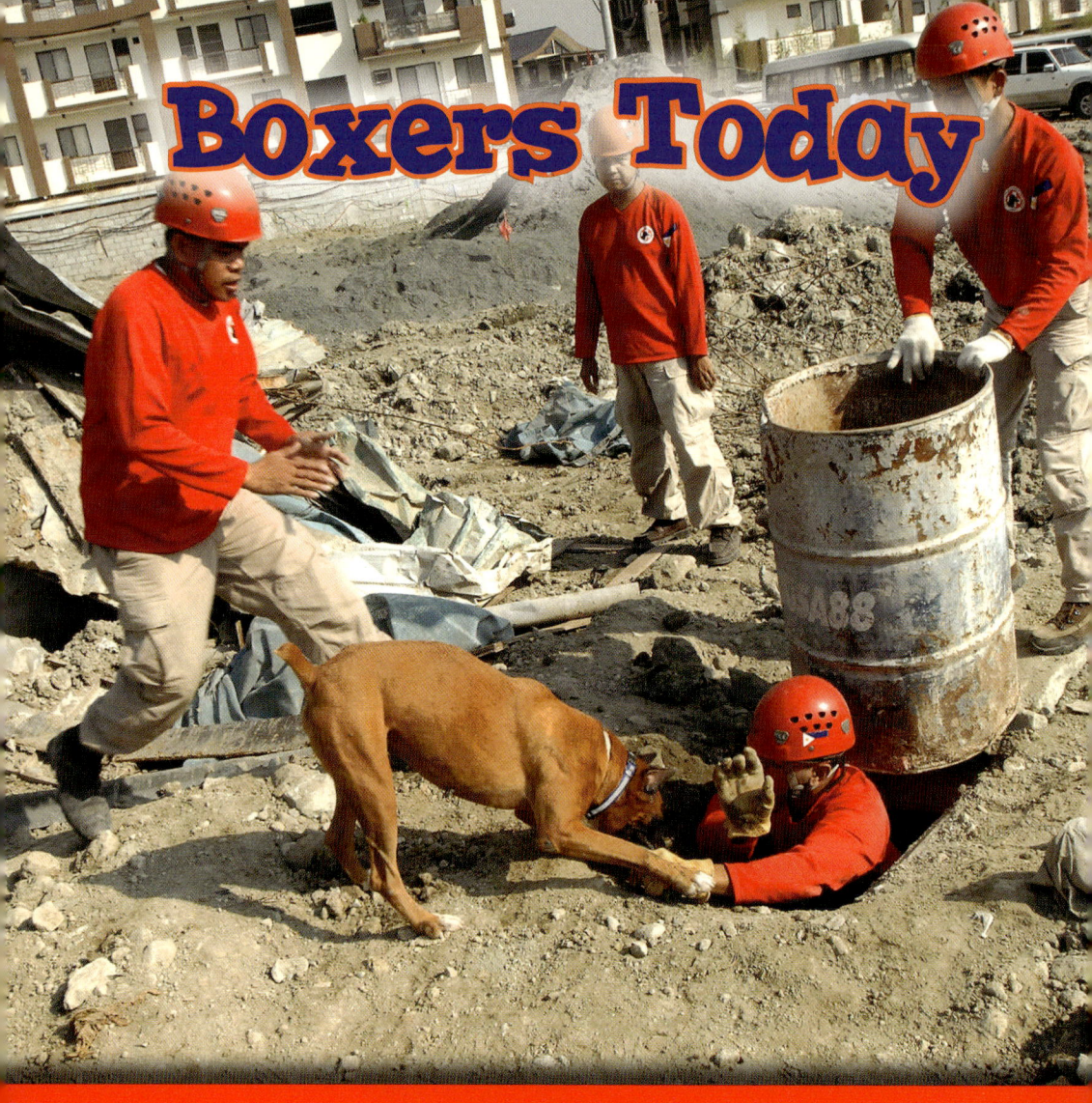

The Boxer is a member of the group of dogs called **working dogs**. Boxers are strong and very intelligent. They make good rescue dogs, police dogs, and guard dogs.

Some Boxers are service dogs that help people with disabilities. Service dogs learn to do jobs that their disabled owners can't do. They may fetch objects, open doors, and turn lights on and off. They may be guide dogs for people who are blind.

fun fact

Some owners put jackets on their Boxers when they have to take them out in the cold.

Boxers are good at learning new skills. They do well in the sport of **agility**. An agility course is like a playground for dogs. It has tunnels, ramps, and high jumps. Owners teach Boxers how to run quickly through the course.

fun fact

Nobody knows for certain how Boxers got their name. The name may come from their habit of punching the air with their paws to play or get attention.

Boxers are very active. They like to run, fetch balls, and catch Frisbees. Many Boxers twirl around and chase their tails when they are happy.

Boxers have a long history of helping people. They are great helpers, pets, and friends.

Glossary

agility—a dog sport where dogs run through a series of obstacles

airways—the paths that air takes from the nose or mouth to the lungs

ancestor—a family member who lived long ago

breed—a type of dog

brindle—brown with black stripes or spots

coat—the hair or fur of an animal

extinct—when every member of a species has died off

fawn—tan, brown, or reddish in color

muzzle—the nose, jaws and mouth of an animal

panting—breathing quickly with an open mouth; dogs cool their bodies by panting.

veterinarian—a doctor who takes care of animals

working dog—a breed of dog that does jobs to help humans

To Learn More

AT THE LIBRARY
American Kennel Club. *The Complete Dog Book for Kids*. Hoboken, N.J.: John Wiley & Sons, 1996.

Meister, Cari. *Boxers*. Edina, Minn.: Checkerboard Books, 2002.

Sanderson, Jeannette. *War Dog Heroes: True Stories of Dog Courage in Wartime*. New York: Scholastic, 1997.

ON THE WEB
Learning more about Boxers is as easy as 1, 2, 3.

1. Go to www.factsurfer.com

2. Enter "Boxers" into search box.

3. Click the "Surf" button and you will see a list of related web sites.

With factsurfer.com, finding more information is just a click away.

Index

agility, 18
ancestors, 11
breed, 11
brindle, 6, 11
Bullenbeissers, 11, 13
coats, 6, 7
ears, 8
English Bulldog, 12, 13
Europe, 11
fawn, 6
flash, 7
Germany, 12
guard dogs, 12, 16
guide dogs, 17
height, 5
hunting dogs, 11, 12
Mastiff, 12, 13
muzzles, 9
name, 18

panting, 9
police dogs, 16
rescue dogs, 16
service dogs, 17
United States, 15
veterinarian, 8
weather, 9, 17
weight, 5
working dogs, 16
World War I, 14
World War II, 14

The images in this book are reproduced through the courtesy of: Eric Isselee, front cover; Mark Raycroft / Getty Images, pp. 4, 6-7, 8, 14, 15; Karen Givens, p. 5; Margo Harrison, p. 9; SueC, p. 10; Juan Martinez, p. 11; JUNIORS BILDARCHIV / agefotostock, p. 12; Erik Lam, p. 13; AFP / Getty Images, p.16; Willie B. Thomas, p. 17; Iztok Noc, p. 19; ludovic rhodes, p. 20; Gail Shumway / Getty Images, p. 21.